THE BONDI FINZ™

PLANET FIN

S J HOUSE

First published by Story House Publishing in 2019

ISBN: 979-8-6423895-8-4

A catalogue record for this book is available from the National Library of Australia

Artwork by Zoran Zlaticanin

Cover by Zoran Zlaticanin

Layout by House Ink* Publishing

Available as a print and ebook from all good bookstores, Amazon and directly from the author at www.sjhouse.com.au

THE BONDI FINZ™

More Bondi Finz adventures

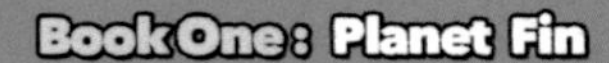

Book One: Planet Fin

Planet Fin's gnarly, alien inhabitants love nothing more than to surf the waves of their oceans. But they did not take care of their environment and the surf turned into a green slimy gunk called slurf. Yuk! They develop a bio beam to rejuvenate the slurf, but the laser misfires. The beam ricochets around the galaxies before zapping Earth through a surf shop window in Bondi, Sydney, Australia, where a row of surfboard fins are displayed. ZAP! KAPOW! The Finz burst to life! Seven knee-high, radical characters begin an epic adventure on a quest for the holy grail of surf.

Will the Finz find out why they were created? Will they help the alien leader to save Planet Fin's surf? Read on, groms! And big groms at heart too!

Book Two: Shark Frog

Have you had your head polished lately? Have you ever been to a surf tailor? With their fins freshly polished and fitted out with new, extravagant rides, the Bondi Finz sure have. They're back again with more surf-mayhem adventures.

Flash finds himself sucked through alien portholes while Mr. Chompy Chomps gets the shock of his shark life. And Bondi's dogs receive an unexpected aggro barney makeover!

A new king is in town and Bondi is about to be attacked by something gnarly, bro! Lord Sarrk and Mode desperately try to stop the invasion.

Will love and a crab-shaped dinner suit save the day!?

Book Three: FreeRacer

Can you say that you love and respect kooks? The Finz might have to. Plastics in the ocean are definitely slowing down the motion! The Finz must find a way to clean the sea and beach and make it plastic-FREE! But this will only happen if Lord Sarrk and Mode can destroy Trevor's gnarly virus and restore Zoid powers in time.

Flash finds himself in a sticky wax dilemma – he needs a FreeForma surf skate bike and makes a surfboard deal with Syke that he cannot keep.

Meanwhile, the race is on. But this is no ordinary competition. Flash and Syke battle it out with the hairy headed humans on the FreeRacer track. Sliding, wave-riding, and freestyling. Who will win? I don't know. Read on to enjoy the show!

Book Four: Surf Subs

Do you speak Dolphinian, bro? More amped Finz antics return where surf subs are go, go, go when the baby Finz spring into action! Bubble wobble on the baby double! Maaaaate!

And just like Jurassic Park, nature finds a way. Eggs have been laid. But by whom? And Flash thinks Eco shark nets are a Rad Power must.

Bone gets a new, one-eyed tooth-crunching buddy while it's shipmates, me hearties! Captain Rhymes sails all the way to Bali... but on a longboard. What!?

Meanwhile, something extraterrestrial has hijacked Flash's surf school and it's definitely NOT shaka, bro! What will happen? I don't know! Read all about it if you want to see the epic conclusion!

Please surf over to my website www.sjhouse.com.au and sign up to my mailing list, where you'll be notified when more Bondi Finz adventures are out and much, much more. I promise, you will not be spammed!

All my best

Simon.

Table of Contents

Chapter Seven
Everybody's got an Inner Aussie Bro

Chapter Eight
Captain Rhymes

Chapter Nine
No More Kooks!

Chapter One
Planet Fin

In another galaxy far, far away, the planet Fin spins in the light of its two suns. It is a strange, alien world populated by life forms with heads and bodies shaped like surfboard fins. Every creature seems to have yellow, bulging, cyclops eyes, sometimes even three eyes, vibrant, colourful skin, gaping jaws, sharp claws, and chomping teeth. And the one thing these peculiar aliens love to do more than anything is to surf planet Fin's luscious, vibrant green waves on some rather peculiar surf contraptions. But sadly, they did not take care of their environment and the surf has slowly turned to SLURF–a gooey slimy gunk.

Under the slime is an aquatic jungle where bizarre alien marine species hunt and swim. A pink octopus with twelve tentacles, three eyes, and a brain for a head, squirts luminous ink. A stingray with horns on its back and eyes on its fins lifts off blue sand while a crab with shark teeth and three eyes on stalks scurries over purple coral. All these creatures live in their own houses and speak to each other in posh English accents.

Today is just like any other day on planet Fin. Alien surfers are out in force, but it's definitely NOT a perfect green slime wave day. It's not surf at all, really. It's slurf.

Daks, one of planet Fin's pro surfers, looms over the slime and surfs as if in slow motion. Daks is bright blue in colour with a sharp fin-shaped head and a cyclops eye. His mono brow slants in an unamused expression as he grunts to other alien surfers, "Nak dak fak lak. This slurf is extra-terrestrially slow today!"

"Sak nak fak lak mhak. This slime's not sick, Daks," cries Larz, one of his mates. "But it certainly looks like it. Look out! Here comes another set of gunk!"

"Rak nak lak fak mhak. Hey! Watch it, bro! Get off my green!" rants a voice behind them from an alien surfer about to be dropped in on.

“Slak nak dak fak lak. This slurf is an outrage!” shouts Daks. All the alien surfers agree, chanting with anger while trying to ride the slime. A bright pink dolphin with three red eyes and a blue horn on its head spins out of the wave. It bleats in agreement, choking on the green, gooey waves.

“Rather disgusting really. It’s playing havoc with my complexion,” the dolphin coughs and splutters before splashing back under.

“Mak dak lak nak. That’s it!” When Daks slaps his surfboard, it lets out a moaning sound as if alive. “I’ve had enough of this gunk! I’m going on strike until something’s done. Everyone, no more Zoids mining until this outrageous slurf turns back to surf. Are you all with me?!”

All the alien surfers jeer in agreement. “Yea-ha!” They punch their clawed fists to the sky chanting, “Mak dak lak. No more Zoids! No more Zoids!” Then they stand on their boards and beat their chests like crazed gorillas.

Deep inside the alien headquarters, Lord Sarrk, the ruler of planet Fin, stands in the control room in front of giant computer screens that show Daks and his fellow surfers chanting in the slurf. Lord Sarrk uses his red dagger claws to nervously type and manipulate all the dials and gadgetry. His bright, pulsing blue skin stands out against his acid green eyes framed by a black, flowing cape. His sidekick, Mode, is an alien sea cucumber that’s bright yellow with leopard spots and three eyes, including one gigantic eye in the centre of his face that is shadowed by a thick mono brow. Mode hovers over Lord Sarrk’s shoulder while they monitor Daks protesting with his surfer mates.

“Mode,” Lord Sarrk worries in a posh English accent, “the slurf is getting increasingly worse by the day. And if these surfers go on strike and stop producing Zoids we'll never gain enough power to increase the Slurf-o-Meter.”

Lord Sarrk and Mode glance at the Slurf-o-Meter on the dashboard. The meter goes from ‘slurf slime’ to ‘surf’, then even higher still to the ultimate ‘Holy Grail of Surf’. But this will only happen if they can improve their ocean environments. The needle points, sadly, to ‘slurf’ only.

“Yikes!” Modes outer eyes pop out on stalks. “We need Zoids! Or the slurf will turn to SLURP! The ultimate wave disaster!”

They look at the Zoid levels on another screen. It measures planet Fin's energy powers and wealth. Zoids are mined deep from within the planet's core where a glowing green crystal is used to power everything or it can be melted down into coins for currency. Right now, the Zoid level needle sits just above ZERO. They're almost depleted.

Seeing this, Lord Sarrk springs into action. “Mode! There's not a moment to lose!” Lord Sarrk frantically flicks switches and turns dials. “It's now or never! We must activate the new bio formula. With one laser blast this biological code could regenerate the oceans, reverse the damage and turn the slurf back to surf!”

Mode's three eyes widen. He raises his mono brow, nodding with approval. He magically morphs an arm to tap at the controls, responding with a robotic voice, “Activating the bio formula, your Greatness!”

An acid green liquid bubbles and hisses, shooting through transparent tubes. Lord Sarrk taps his red talons on a series of buttons to launch a code sequence. He turns random dials then flicks switches in a frenzy. Mode's giant eye follows Sarrk's every movement. He raises his mono brow higher in wide-eyed anticipation.

"Here we go, Mode. This will use up the last of our Zoids. If it doesn't work, then I'm afraid all is lost. Three, two, one!" Lord Sarrk stomps his blue fists on a red fire button. The bio code bursts from the tubes and shoots through pipes. The control room shudders.

High on a cliff overlooking the protesting surfers, a strange telescopic laser machine activates and fires an acid green bio beam ZAP ZAP ZAP Ka-POW! But something goes drastically wrong, the machine switches aim and misses the ocean of slime altogether. It shoots skyward instead. The green beam hits planet Fin's moon. BLAM! Then the beam ricochets off like a stray firework out into deep space.

"Oh no!" Lord Sarrk's eyes widen in horror, watching the disaster unfold on a computer screen. "The machine's malfunctioned!"

"Warning alert! Warning alert!" screams the computer system as panic sirens whirl, sparks spit, and fuzz and green smoke rises from the controls.

Mode's mono brow slants angrily, "You bumbling fool! I told you not to use that old beaming machine!" Mode instantly sprouts arms and legs to grab a nearby fire extinguisher. He blasts pink clouds over the smoking controls.

Lord Sarrk stomps his claw on a loud speaker button, "Attention! All engineers to the control room at once! There's been a major malfunction in the system! The bio beam has gone rogue!"

Lord Sarrk and Mode helplessly grapple to correct the situation. Bizarre alien engineers that wear intelligent specs and white lab coats race to their aid, but the Slurf-o-Meter drops to ZERO and releases an exhausted sound.

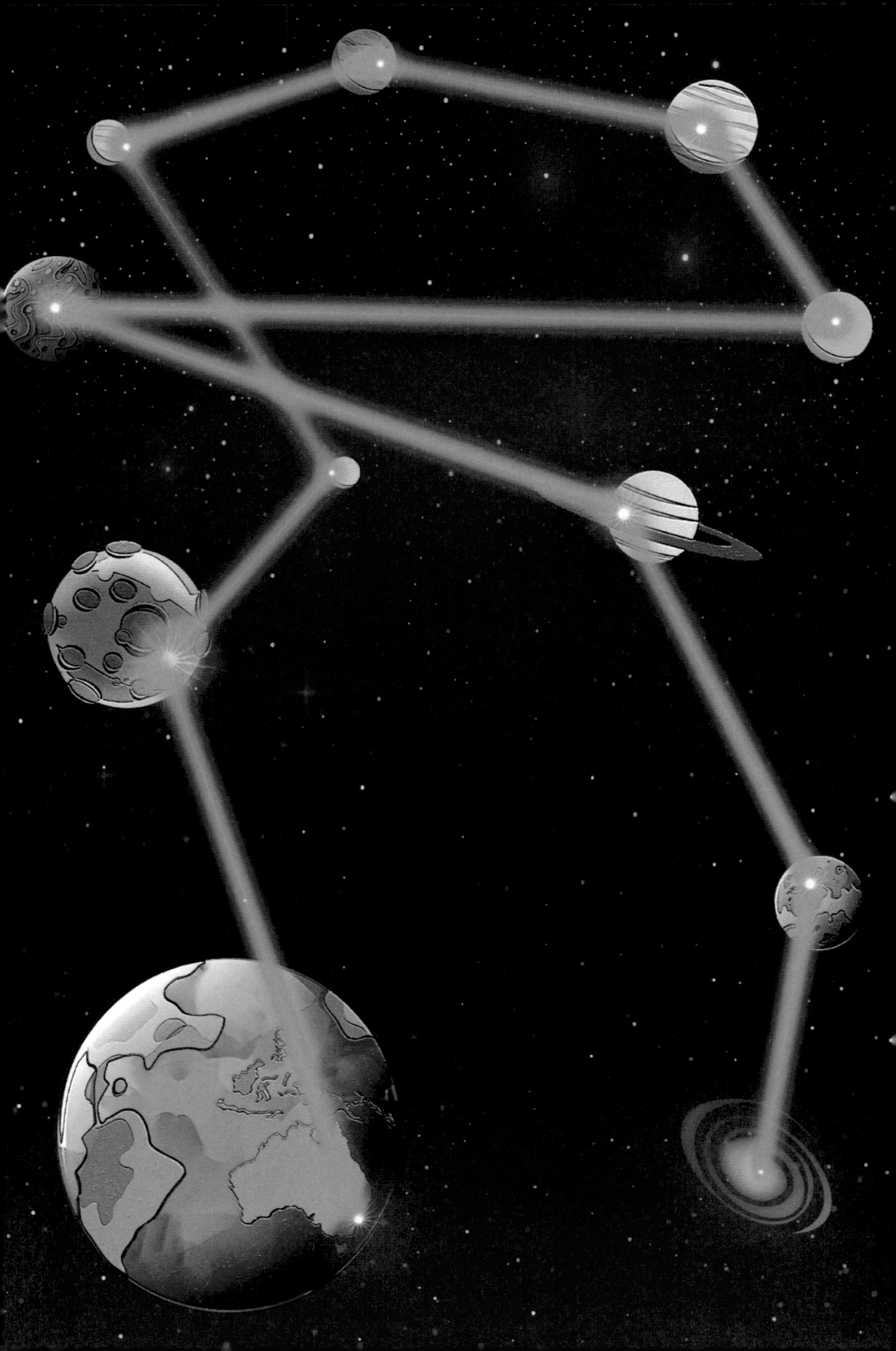

The bio beam appears from a black hole vortex. The fabric of space time has altered its code. The beam bounces around the galaxies, ricochets off planets, stars, and moons until it finally hits Earth's moon. KA-BOOM! The alien bio beam charges directly down onto planet Earth. ZOID! ZOID! ZOID! The beam hits Australia, the coast of Sydney, firing directly through a Bondi beach surf shop window. Zap! Zap! Zap!

SURF SHOP
SHANES SURF SHOP
LET'S GO SURFING
OPEN

The surf shop ignites in a magical beam of alien, acid green light that narrows onto a surfboard fins display. For some unknown extra-surfy-terrestrial reason, the fins BURST TO LIFE! They magically sprout arms and legs while mouths and eyes pop open. The creatures jump off their window display onto the surf shop floor. They stare around in wide-eyed amazement like kids in a toy shop. The Bondi Finz are born!

LET'S GO
SURFING

"Hey?"

"What the...?"

"Maaaate?"

"Woooo, sick Bro!?"

Everything else in the surf shop twinkles and sparkles in a magical smoky haze. Instinctively, the Finz grab hold of shrunken surfboards and run out the door to the beach.

Chapter Two
The Finz

ONE YEAR LATER...

It's a bright, beautiful, sunny morning at Bondi beach and the waves are rolling in and crashing on golden sands while seagulls cry. A dog pees on a lamppost while kids whiz by on skateboards. The Finz, who have been settling into their new Bondi home, appear to have been accepted by the human, hairy headed world going on above them.

Flash is a bright orange fin with black lightning strikes etched down his sides. He's the natural leader of the group and is always seeking adventure. Bone is a cool looking D fin, black in colour with white pinstripes down the sides. He's tough and doesn't suffer fools gladly.

"Hey Flash," nods Bone, "how's it hanging, man?"

"Good, Bone mate! Hanging ten, you know. Toes to the nose."

"Did you see that colourful lightning this morning, Flash?" Bone points to the clouds. "The whole sky lit up like a Christmas tree and then one of the fins on my board spoke to me!"

"What?" Flash jumps back in surprise.

Bone shrugs his shoulders, "It sure did, man."

Flash is about to ask more, but the sound of an electric engine cuts him off. Syke zooms in on a surf skate bike. Vroom, vroom! The bike is super rad with a surfboard seat and large fin on the back attached to a giant kryptonic skateboard wheel. Syke is bright yellow in colour with palm tree patterns. He thinks he's the coolest and wears wooden shades that he never takes off... ever!

"Hey Bone, hey Flash!" Syke jumps off his bike and kicks the stand. The Finz admire it.

"Sick ride, Syke!"

"Thanks Bone. I'm taking it to the skate bowl now."

"But how did you get one of these your size, Syke?" Flash shakes his head in disbelief. "Aren't they only for humans? The hairy heads?" Flash points up to the passing feet and legs above him.

"I don't know, man. I found it outside the surf shop this morning already to go."

"Hmm, this IS weird," Flash thinks out loud, rubbing his chin. "First, Bone's fin talks to him and now this."

Sharp rocks up to Bone, Flash and Syke with his surfboard tucked under his arm. Sharp is Japanese, his fin is white with red stripes, and he sports a goatee beard. Sharp is the wise, free thinker of the group, even if the other Finz don't really understand what he means most of the time. "Arr, hey dudes," Sharp smiles with a wave.

"Hey Sharp mate," replies the group.

"How were the waves, Sharp? Did anything strange happen to your board?" asks Flash.

"Arr, I don't know, man," Sharp grins, pointing, "I think you'd better ask Woody."

The Finz's eyes pop open with surprise, "What?"

Woody, a wood-grained fin with a cheesy grin, rocks up to the others with a surfboard sticking out of his behind.

The Finz crack up. "Oh no, Woody," Flash points, laughing. "Have you been trying to nose ride short boards?"

Woody grins, shrugging his shoulders, "I don't know why, but I thought I had it at one point, man." Woody looks over his shoulder at the surfboard sticking out of his bum while the others laugh out loud.

"No, but seriously guys," Sharp cuts in, "my inner-wave chi must be outstanding today because the wave I was just riding actually grew a face and smiled at me!"

"What the...?" Flash exclaims with concern.

Sharp nods and points at the ocean. "Crazy, right? And that's not the half of it, bros! MJ and Jazz are out there right now with some freaky looking extra-terrestrial fish too!"

The Finz watch in surprise as MJ surfs alongside a bright blue dolphin that leaps from the waves and spins through the air. It has six jagged dorsal fins running down its back and eyes on stalks with a red horn on its nose. It makes a strange, alien bleating cry. MJ is astonished when the dolphin speaks in a posh accent. "Good morning! A glorious day for a swim, isn't it? This ocean feels divine on my skin."

MJ, also known as Mary Joy, carves up another wave as she chases neon green Manta Rays with bright red eyes on the end of their acid green wings. The rays fly across the surface of the water. MJ is Chinese with a beautiful rose pattern on her body. She loves nature and cares for the environment. She smiles at Jazz. "This is so cool. But where are they coming from!? I've never seen any of these species at Bondi before." The alien sea creatures disappear back under the waves.

Jazz is a white-coloured fin with a frangipani floral design. She's smart, fearless, and always up for adventure. She punches her fist to the sky and shouts out to the others, "Akaw! This is totally awesome guys! We're riding freestyle."

"Come on, guys," cries Flash. "Let's investigate these slippery invaders." Flash leads the charge and the Finz grab their boards to race down the sand to the water.

Woody waddles with the board stuck in his behind. He shouts as he runs, "Hey fellas, wait up!"

Suddenly, they all stop in their tracks when they hear a snarl at their feet then gnashing sounds. A pulsing red crab with three bulging eyes on stalks and fanged teeth snips by them. It opens its jaws wide while blasting out an ear splitting "ROARRRRR!"

Humans scream and shout, pointing at the strange creature. The alien crab breathes in the wonderful fresh air of Bondi. “Good day to you all. I’m Trevor. A beautiful day for a sideways stroll along the beach, hey?” Then, more alien monster crabs appear.

“What’s going on?” the Finz ask. Flash stares around in amazement. “Bondi’s being invaded by talking alien marine species!”

Without warning, acid green lightning flickers over the Finz, followed by a clap of green rumbling thunder. A booming, godly voice emanates from the clouds, “Flash!” “Can you hear me, Flash?”

Flash looks to the sky in astonishment. Then he turns to his Finz buddies that are frozen stiff. He stares back up at the sky in sheer amazement like he’s hearing God’s voice. He trembles, “Hello? Who is that? Who are you? And bro, what have you done to my mates?”

Chapter Three
Space time pathway

Flash stands on the sand staring up at the sky waiting for a response. Back on planet Fin, Lord Sarrks in the control room with Mode while they communicate with Flash, observing him on their monitor screens. Lord Sarrk's voice booms from the clouds, "I am Lord Sarrk from planet Fin in another galaxy far, far away. A space time pathway has opened and connected our worlds. I have been observing you and your finny friends all morning."

Flash squints up into the sky astonished. "Lord Sarrk? Planet what, bro?"

"I am your father, Flash," replies Lord Sarrk in a stern tone.

Mode's eyes pop and swivel at Lord Sarrk. His mono brow lifts in surprise muttering to himself, "Double yikes!"

Flash is totally shocked. He stutters, "M-my, my father?" "But... but...how...?"

"I created a bio laser beam to save our oceans because we did not take care of our planet. But something went drastically wrong. It went rogue, bouncing around the galaxies until it finally reached Earth, zapping you and your friends. Somehow, it instantly brought you to life."

"Laser beams? Biology codes?" Flash questions with excitement. "That's...way cool. But how did you damage your oceans, Lord Sarrk?"

"Please, call me Sarrk or L'Sarrk, if you're feeling homie that is. The problem is, we wrapped our products in Slak Rak Mak and discarded it into our oceans. Sadly, it has turned our surf to slurf."

"Slak Rak what, bro!? That totally sucks L'Sarrk. Slurf?"

"The bio laser was designed to reverse the slurf slime. It rejuvenates the genetics of the marine species and returns it back to surf."

Flash stares back out at the sea, pondering what he's heard, "Ahh, this must explain the alien marine species?"

Lord Sarrk continues, "The experiment failed and we had thought all was lost. But the space time pathway re-opened and the bio beam returned. It ignited into the controls in the beaming chamber and brought everything back on-line. Now our two worlds are connected. Flash, my son, it's time for you to come home."

"What the...? Mate! Home? Bondi's my home L'Sarrk! This is where I live with me mates!"

"Flash, you and your finny friends must return to planet Fin at once! The human world is no place for pointy bros such as yourselves. And we have much to learn about your creation."

Tears form in Flash's eyes, "But, but, the hairy heads have accepted us. We get along fine. Sure, they might drop in on our waves now again but hey, we love those greasy mops going on above us. And besides, bro, where do you get off telling me I've got to beam back to God knows where and become some sort of alien experiment! No way, Jose!"

Lord Sarrk's voice gets very serious, "Flash, I am your father and you will do exactly what I tell you to do now."

Suddenly, Lord Sarrk is cut off when a fierce monster crab roars and terrorizes humans. Flash sees people panicking as more bizarre sea creatures with posh English accents invade Bondi beach. He argues back, "L'Sarrk mate, what about all these alien sea beasts terrorizing my neighbourhood! Hmm? Have you thought about that?"

Lord Sarrk tries to remain calm as he explains, "Flash, random portholes have opened. One was under our ocean. Planet Fin's marine species have been vortexed to Earth. We need them back urgently or the slurf will get even worse and turn to slurp."

"Slurp? That doesn't sound good, me old mate!"

Lord Sarrk sighs, "It's the ultimate wave disaster." Mode nods in agreement eagerly watching Flash on the screen.

Flash sees a monster crab now hanging off a human's toe. The crab waves to him, roaring, "Pleased to meet you. My name is Trevor."

Flash's eyes dart to the ocean where he sees jellyfish with glowing brains for heads. They're singing loudly and totally out of tune. Humans run up the beach, covering their ears and screaming for help.

Lord Sarrk watches the commotion on his screen. "Flash, there's no time to lose. You must return these creatures to planet Fin at once! Will you help us?

Flash takes in the chaos around him as well as Lord Sarrk's pleading tone. He nods his head in agreement, "Okay! But bro, how? I mean, I'll help, but only if we can stay on Earth."

Lord Sarrk ponders Flash's request. "Here's how you can help. Now that we are connected, I can beam you the Power of Fin. With this power, you will be able to reverse the vortex and send the alien invaders back to us."

Flash stares at his mates who are frozen like statues. "And what about my mates? They're as stiff as stand-up paddle boarders, bro."

"Yeah, um, that's a technical difficulty. We're working on it. For now, just try the Power of Fin."

Lord Sarrk turns dials in a frenzy on his control panel. Mode's brow narrows while he hovers over Sarrk's shoulder to make sure he doesn't make any mistakes this time. He snaps at him, "No! Sequence code F, not G! You'll zap him into oblivion." Mode sprouts arms again, making the proper corrections.

Back on Bondi beach, Flash gasps in astonishment, "The power of what? Mate? Fin? I don't know about this, bro!"

Lord Sarrk explains, "Yes, you will be given a great power. You must punch your fist to the sky and say: By the Power of Fin I will send these alien invaders home! Do it now!"

Flash hears more cries of panic around him. Humans are shouting for help. He shrugs his shoulders thinking he has nothing to lose. He punches his fist in the air as Lord Sarrk told him to and yells out, "BY THE POWER OF FIN I WILL SEND THESE ALIEN INVADERS HOME!"

In an instant, acid green lightning strikes down from the sky and zaps his fist. It ignites his body with electricity. Zap! Zap! Zap! Buzz! Ka-POW!

Flash is staggered by what has just happened to him. He stares at his fist, then back up to the sky as a new, magical energy force flows within him.

Lord Sarrk's voice commands him loudly, "Now, go forth, oh young and brave fin warrior. With the Power of Fin you will be able to overcome many obstacles. And great things will come to you." The colour of the sky changes and then Lord Sarrk's voice fades away.

Flash starts to panic, "Hey! Wait! Come back..." But Lord Sarrk has gone.

Flash looks at his fist with wonder. He punches it to the sky again to see if the power still works and shouts, "BY THE POWER OF FIN!" An acid green laser shoots from his fist. There's a gawping sound above him and a seagull drops at his feet. "Oops! That's not cool." Flash glances up and down the beach to make sure no one's watching. Then he points his fist at the seagull and says, "By the Power of Fin! Bring this gull back to life!" The acid green laser shines over the seagull and instantly brings it back to life.

The seagull squawks, "Maaaate!" flying away unharmed.

Flash's face lights up in amazement. "Sick! I've got "RAD-POWER!"

Chapter Four
The Rad Power of Fin!

The other Finz burst back to life as if nothing has happened. Flash gushes with relief, "Thank goodness, you're back!"

Bone shrugs, "Back? We didn't go anywhere, man."

"Yeah, Flash mate, back from where?" Woody asks scratching his head.

Flash is just about to tell them everything when the Finz hear the alien cries and the awful out-of-tune singing coming from the jellyfish. Flash frets, "Ah, forget it. I'll explain later."

A human shouts, running past them, "Somebody do something quickly! I can't take any more of this!"

The Finz look to Flash for answers. He tells them with a friendly but commanding tone, "Guys, there's no time to lose. We need to send these slippery invaders back home. I'll take care of the ones in the ocean with MJ and Jazz, you lot deal with the ones on land." The Finz agree and Flash bolts off down the sand to the sea.

Then Syke thinks about it a bit more and wonders, "Take care how, man?"

Sharp calls after Flash, "Arr, is that a good brainwave, Flash? You must channel your inner-wave more, arr."

An alien crab roars at their feet and tries to snip Woody's toe. He cries out, dodging the serrated claws, "What's the deal? Are you out of your fin-box mate? Argh!"

"Come on, guys. They're just crabs!" shouts Flash.

"Yeah right! With gnarly, giant shark teeth!" Bone pleads, avoiding Trevor's jaws.

Trevor roars at Bone, "I brush every day, don't you know."

Flash jumps in the water and paddles out to Jazz and MJ, who have been having fun in the waves.

"This is amazing, Flash," Jazz calls out to him. "Meet Beatrice. Isn't she cute?" Flash waves hello as Beatrice, the alien dolphin, bleats and batts her eyelashes, spinning out of a wave.

MJ paddles over, "And these jellyfish colours are so awesome, but their voices? Not so much." The sound of the singing jellyfish is unbearable. MJ covers her ears.

Flash shakes his head, "Guys, we have to send them back. They can't stay."

Jazz frowns, "Send them back where?"

Beatrice leaps from a wave and bleats sadly, "Not back to that gunky slime on planet Fin, I hope. Please. It plays havoc with my complexion."

"Yeah, Flash, why?" MJ surfs playfully alongside Beatrice. "We're having so much fun."

Flash explains, "Because they don't belong here, MJ. They're needed in another ocean and if they don't return that ocean will die. Surely you understand."

MJ thinks about Flash's comment. "You mean like the parrot fish? And how important they are to our reefs here?"

"Exactly! Without parrot fish, the reefs would die."

Jazz and MJ look sadly at Beatrice and the singing jellyfish. "We'll miss you guys, but you have to go home."

MJ turns back to Flash. "What's the plan, Flash? How do we do it?"

"Yeah, Flash," Jazz wonders aloud, "send them how?"

Back on planet Fin, Lord Sarrk and Mode watch and listen to the Finz from the control room. Computers flash and dials flicker in an array of lights. "Mode, there's no time to lose, The Finz need to go aquatic. You know what to do!"

Mode nods and slants his mono brow with determination. He sprouts hands and types in a launching sequence. "Activating surf-subs, your Greatness. Initiating Baby Finz!" He flicks switches and presses buttons, then turns one final dial.

"Excellent thinking, Mode," Lord Sarrk beams, rubbing his red-clawed blue hands in approval.

Back on Bondi, there is a clap of magical acid green thunder, and lightning flickers in the sky. Flash shudders when a laser beam strikes down from the clouds. It hits the Finz's surfboards and transforms them into surf-submarines. Glass bubbles encase them inside and then they dive under the ocean.

Flash can't believe his eyes. "What the...? What's happening to our boards? More Rad Power from the alien planet? I can't steer this thing!" Flash grapples to control the surf-sub, pulling on the steering wheel. He pushes the foot pedals then notices a big red FIRE button in the centre of his control panel with the words 'Rad Power' next to it. His face lights up. "Cooooooool!"

Jazz and MJ are amazed at their surf-subs, too. "Amped!" shouts Jazz inside her sub bubble. "Surfboard submarines. This is so epic!"

"Way Epic!" MJ nods, hearing Jazz's voice inside her glass bubble. "The ocean is so beautiful from down here too."

Alien monster fish with eyes on the end of tentacles smile as they swim past them. Flash stares wide-eyed at MJ and Jazz's surf-subs whizzing by. Cute little Baby Finz are fixed underneath their surfboards, blowing bubbles to propel the surf-subs forward. Flash smiles as he realizes. "So that's where our subs get their power from. Baby Finz!" Flash gives them the thumbs up. But then he does a double-take when he hears the Baby Finz talking in their own bubble language.

"Bubble wobble double!" orders Baby Fin Yellow. "Let's help them round up these slippery ET's!"

"Bubble wobble lubbery, you got it!" salutes Baby Fin Blue. "I'll head for the jellyfish. You take the stingrays."

"Bubble wobble fobble, wait up!" Shouts Baby Fin Orange. "Does that mean I get the alien sharks?"

"Wobble double wooble," calls back Baby Fin Blue. "Don't be a wuss! And besides, you blew our cover this morning!"

Flash stares in awe. "This is totally crazy off-the-charts gnarly! It must be the work of the aliens. Bone's fin did talk!" He watches MJ and Jazz speed off after the alien fish. The Baby Finz are determined to catch them all.

Flash suddenly sees an alien monster groper swim in front of him. He stomps on the fire button and shouts "RAD POWER." An acid green laser shoots from his surf-sub and the giant groper gawps then gets zapped up into a vortex. "Gnarly!" Flash smiles, then races after more species. He zooms under the ocean like a pro and shouts orders from inside his sub-bubble to MJ and Jazz.

With the help of the Baby Finz, MJ and Jazz round up the alien marine species in their surf-subs like they're sheep herders. They tackle the bizarre alien creatures together, then steer them in front of Flash who shouts, "RAD POWER!" Green lasers shoot from his surf-sub and zap the aliens away. The creatures rise out of the sea in a sparkly green whirlpool. They chat to themselves as they get swallowed up in the vortex. It sucks them back up into space and beyond. But little does anyone know that something sinister is lurking in the shadows, with a monstrous bite...

Chapter Five
Mr. Chompy Chomps

Lord Sarrk and Mode watch in amazement while the alien species hit the vortex and planet Fin's Zoid levels increase. The lights on their computers flash green like winning points in a game. Mode sprouts hands and places them on his head in disbelief. "Your Greatness, the Finz's actions are increasing power levels!"

Lord Sarrk smiles, "Their positive actions on Earth are having a positive effect on our planet too, Mode! They're earning us Zoids!"

Mode points, "Look! The Slurf-o-Meter! It's moving too!"

Back on the golden sands of Bondi, Bone, Sharp, Woody and Syke continue to try and round up the alien creatures on the beach. But it's not an easy task. The creatures keep nipping and pinching our heroes with their claws and sharp teeth.

"Argh! Yikes, maaaaate!" Syke shouts with a crab hanging off his toe. "These crabs are aggro, barney mate!"

"Arr, this is not crab-tastic," whines Sharp as he tries to avoid a snapping pincer.

"I hate these gnarly nippers, man!" Bone yells while he holds one up that slices at his face.

"Put me down at once, you imbecile! I'll have your fins for this!" The monster crab continues to snip and snap at him.

Meanwhile, back under the ocean, a great white shark is being chased by an alien monster shark. The alien shark is twice the size of the great white, with six gnarly dorsal fins, horns on its head, a cyclops eye, and giant fangs hanging from its jaws. It's about to bite the great white in two. Flash has to make a split-second decision. He takes aim with great precision so as not to harm the great white. "I wouldn't want to zap him by accident," Flash says to himself, then shoots from his sub. The great white shark YELPS with fear. Zap! Ka-POW!

Flash hits the alien shark just in the nick of time. It zaps from the ocean in a green explosion, rising to the sky and into outer space through the vortex. But just before he disappears, the alien shark shrugs apologetically, "Terribly sorry, old bean, but one must eat, you know." And, zap! He's gone.

The great white that Flash just saved flicks on his fins, charging towards Flash with a gaping maw. To Flash's horror, his surf-sub suddenly glitches, changing back to a normal surfboard again. He's totally exposed under the ocean! Jazz and MJ gasp and race to protect him from the shark that's about to bite him in two. "OH NO!" they scream.

Back in the control room, Lord Sarrk points at the screen. "We've lost power on Flash's surf-sub!"

"Yikes!" Mode's three eyes pop out on stalks. "Another glitch in the system! It must be a virus. I am trying to fix it now." Lord Sarrk stands aside to let Mode grapple at the controls.

Under the ocean, Flash is frozen with fear. The great white opens its jaws wide. Flash covers his face… and a giant slurping tongue slaps all over him. Flash opens his scrunched-up eyes. The great white is thanking him for saving his life by slurping his tongue all over Flash's face. The great white is like a giant puppy dog. Flash laughs with relief. He tickles the great white's gills. The shark enjoys the fuss and they instantly bond. The great white chomps his jaws playfully.

"Ha ha ha," Flash laughs. "That tickles, huh? Pleased to meet you, boy. I'm going to call you...Mr. Chompy Chomps!" MJ and Jazz watch from their sub-bubbles and smile with relief.

The shark gnashes his teeth together with approval of his new name. He snaps and snarls, but to Flash's surprise, he can actually understand what Chompy is saying. "What's that, boy? You're hungry? There's not enough fish in the ocean to eat anymore? The humans are taking all the fish away?"

Chompy nods and whines like a puppy dog. Flash thinks pensively, rubbing his chin. He can hear L'Sarrk's voice echo inside his mind... *The Power of Fin...*"Hmm, I wonder..."

Moments later, Flash emerges from the waves, surfing back to shore. MJ and Jazz's surf-subs bob to the surface and transform back to surfboards again. They ride a wave in and high five each other.

MJ shouts, "That was radical with a capital R!"

"You said it, surf sister!" Jazz calls back.

Mr. Chompy Chomps pops his head out of the ocean and grins widely with a large prize tuna in his mouth. Flash has rejuvenated the ocean from over-fishing. Chompy now has more food. But no time to celebrate just yet. Flash sees the other Finz stumble by in a panic with the crabs still biting them.

"Argh! Flash mate, get these oversized crustaceans off us quickly!"

The monster crabs roar and snarl. Flash punches his fist in the air, "By the Power of Fin send these monster crabs home!" A zap of green light circles on the crabs, vortexing them up into the sky and beyond.

"Arr, that was truly surf-chi-tastic, Flash! Surf angels are at work here."

"Not surf angels, Sharp! RAD POWER!"

The sky ignites again with acid green thunder. Lord Sarrk's booming voice rings out. "Flash, my son, a strange phenomenon has happened. When you vortexed our marine species and rejuvenated the fish, you increased Zoid power here on planet Fin. And the Slurf-o-Meter moved!"

Flash's eyes light up with excitement. "Really? That's awesome with a capital 'A', L'Sarrk, me old mate!"

"Yes, Flash. It appears that we are truly connected. And if this continues, you might eventually improve our oceans and turn the Surf-o-Meter to 'surf'. And maybe one day, you just might earn us all the right to get to the Holy Grail of Surf!"

"The Holy Grail of Surf? Mate! What's that?"

"An epic surf adventure. A paradise on waves. Do you and your finny friends want to go there?"

"Yes! Yes! We do!"

"Then you can stay on Earth to help the human's environment and continue to do good."

Flash punches his fist to the sky. "RAD POWER!"

Back on planet Fin, Lord Sarrk and Mode watch the Finz on their giant computer screen while they surf and have fun on Bondi beach. Everything has returned to normal.

"Well done, Mode, for zapping that great white shark Mr. Chompy Chomps into a friendly in the nick of time!"

"I had to act in nano-seconds, your Greatness. If I hadn't, Flash would have been fin-food."

"Perhaps the creation of the Finz was no random accident after all. And maybe I have gotten something right for once. Now, before we forget, we must neutralize the humans' memories on Bondi beach so that they don't remember any of this strange, alien phenomenon ever taking place." Lord Sarrk types codes into the machines, turning knobs and dials every which way. Suddenly, a machine explodes. It ignites in green smoke, warning alarms sound.

Mode shrieks, "You've overloaded the system. That's the second time today."

Bizarre alien engineers race into the control room. "My Lord, you had better come quickly. Something is transporting from the beaming chamber."

Lord Sarrk grimaces, "Oh no, no, no, no! What have I done now?"

Mode sprouts legs. "Triple Yikes! To the beaming chamber!" Everyone races out of the control room.

On Bondi beach, Flash shouts, "RAD POWER!" All the Finz and humans enjoy the surf. Trevor the Alien crab quietly snips past with his shifty three eyes. It appears that not ALL of the alien invaders have gone.

Chapter Six
It's Flat!

The sun rises fast out of the ocean to meet the sky. It's going to be another beautiful day at Bondi. A pod of dolphins skims across calm waters while a fishing boat chases the morning light surrounded by a flock of hungry gulls. On dry land at the Finz's surf shop headquarters, the Finz are all waking up. The early morning sun casts a magical haze through the surf shop window shining its warm rays over their display. Flash is up first with a big stretch and yawn.

"Hey, morning guys." Flash jumps off the display.

"Morning Flash." Bone rubs his eyes.

Syke flicks on his shades. "Flash mate!"

"Arr, good morning, Flash, arr, the surf chi does not feel good today arr." Sharp does some kung-fu moves then strokes his goatee beard.

Woody stares out the window and across the beach to a sparkling flat ocean. "Sharp's right, me old finny mates. It's a beautiful day alright, but there's no waves." Woody and the Finz stare out the window to a beautiful, twinkling blue but flat sea.

LET'S GO
SURFING

"Bummer man. Now what?" Bone groans. They look at each other with disappointed faces.

The surf shop door swings open with a chiming sound and in walks MJ and Jazz followed by loud snipping noises. Jazz smiles, "Morning guys. Another beautiful day out there. We just took Trevor for a sideways walk." Trevor, the bright red alien crab with shark teeth, roars like a lion then swivels his three eyes on stalks happily.

"A delightful morning stroll, ladies. The fresh air on this planet is simply divine."

The Finz reply with sullen tones, "Oh, hey, morning Jazz, morning MJ."

Flash pats Trevor's shell, "Shouldn't we be sending Trevor back to his planet by now? I could get into a lot of trouble, you know."

Trevor whines, gnashing his claws in protest.

"Awe, can't we keep him for a little longer?" Jazz pleads. "He's good company and his nippers are super handy."

Trevor reveals a fizzy drink and cuts it open with his nippers like a can opener. He hands it to Jazz, then offers a packet of crisps, snipping off the top for MJ.

"Lobster flavour, madam," Trevor grins, bearing enormous fangs.

"Trevor, you're such a sweetie." MJ pats his shell, munching on the crisps. Trevor roars so loudly that the surf shop window vibrates.

Shane, the surf shop owner, who appears to also be under some sort of alien spell, shouts from the till, "Hey guys! Keep it down!

And no man-eating crabs in the store. Haven't you seen the sign outside?"

The Finz groan, looking at a sign that clearly says no man-eating crabs allowed in the store. Flash shrugs, "Sorry, Shane."

MJ pats Trevor's shell again, "What's the matter with you guys? Why all the sad faces?"

"Yeah, what's up?" Jazz asks, guzzling down her fizzy drink.

"There's no waves," Flash sighs.

"Yeah man, it's flat as sand," Bone huffs.

MJ laughs at the boys, "Come on guys, there's more to life than just surfing every day, right?

"Yeah," agrees Jazz, "like I heard there's going to be no waves all week."

The Finz look at each other with disgusted faces. Trevor mumbles with contempt.

"No waves all week!?" Syke bursts into uncontrollable tears.

MJ giggles, holding her hand to her lips, "Come on, Syke, let's think of something else we can do."

"Yeah, Syke," consoles Jazz.

Syke continues to sob, "No waves all week, man!" His tears pool in his sunglasses then around his bare feet. The Finz stare at the floor in pensive thought.

"I got it!" Jazz clicks her fingers. "What about FreeRacer? We could go check out the new surf skate track!"

“Arr, it’s closed for maintenance. The wave machine has lost its surf chi powers.” The Finz roll their eyes at Sharp.

“Even the surf track’s flat?” Woody raises his brows.

“I’m afraid so, guys.”

Trevor holds his claws over his eyes in sadness. The Finz look to the floor again and sigh. The room falls silent.

“What about going for a skate?” Woody pipes up. “Hitting the concrete waves.”

The Finz cheer up and nod in agreement.

“We can’t today,” MJ frowns. “Jazz and I just walked past the skate bowl this morning and it’s under construction. They’re repairing the cement.” All the Finz groan.

Syke continues to sob. “Nothing’s going right, man. What are we going to do? We’re supposed to be Finz. We surf, we skate, we ride. Are we supposed to just sit in this surf shop all day watching wax melt?”

“Arr, we could surf-meditate, Syke, so the surf angels will answer our calling and bring the wave gods back, arr.” They look at each other, confused by Sharp’s suggestion. Trevor rotates his three eyes.

Suddenly, Flash’s face lights up, he snaps his fingers with a bright idea in his head. “I’ve got it, guys! What about starting a band? We always talk about becoming musicians, right? Well, if there aren’t any waves then this is the perfect opportunity.” The Finz look at each other with excitement in their eyes.

Syke wipes his tears and his snivelling nose. "That's a beautiful idea, bro!" The others nod in agreement. Trevor snaps his pincers, making a castanet sound.

"Arr Flash, arr, there's only one problem with this surf-tastic awesome idea of yours, arr,"

"What's that, Sharp?"

"Arr, we don't have any instruments to practice with bro, arr."

"Yeah, Flash, Sharp's right. We got no sounds, man," shrugs Woody.

The Finz stare at each other, nodding in agreement. A lost feeling comes over them again. Syke bursts back into tears. Trevor scuttles over to console him with a gentle nip.

"Nothing's going right, man. Nothing! I feel so down and sad!" Trevor gently nudges Syke's foot then snips open a box of tissues, handing them over. Syke takes one, violently blowing his nose.

The surf shop falls silent once more with yet another dilemma. The sound of Syke's sobbing continues.

"I've got it!" Bone smacks his fist into his palm. "How about we head down to the music shop? We could use the instruments in there. Try before you buy, right?" The Finz smile, snapping out of their gloom.

"That's a fin-tastic idea, Bone!" Syke dries his eyes, smiling.

"To the music shop! Let's go!" Flash marches out the door. The others jump off their display, running outside to follow him. Trevor scuttles after them roaring happily.

A woman points at Trevor on the street and screams.

“Excuse me, madam, I’m terribly sorry,” winks Trevor, snipping by.

The woman screams again, “Arrrgh! A talking crab!”

Trevor sighs, rolling his eyes, “Oh pull yourself together, madam. Here, have a crab stick!” He offers her a tasty crab stick to munch, but the woman faints.

Chapter Seven
Everybody's got an Inner Aussie Bro

At the music shop called Bummed-Note, random sounds are heard of humans playing badly while they practice throughout the store. A guitar twangs while a saxophone blasts scales out of tune, and a drum bangs off-beat. Human feet and legs pass by the Finz while they look up to giant-sized instruments on display.

"Awe mate, how are we ever going to afford any of these? Look how expensive these sick guitars are." Flash does a double-take, staring at the price tags.

"Remember, Flash, we're not buying today. We're just trying," Jazz reminds him.

Sharp stares up at a set of drums, stroking his moustache. "Arr, never mind being able to afford these instruments arr, what about being able to reach them? We're way too small for these human, hairy headed instruments." Sharp reaches for a large snare drum but is unable to get his hands to the top.

Bone stands next to a bass guitar that's more than five times his height. "Yeah man, how are we going to jam with these?"

"And guys, look how tall these microphone stands are. How will we ever sing into these?" MJ reaches for the mic, but can't come close to touching it.

All the Finz stare up at the giant human instruments, scratching their heads with disappointment. It seems that the day is doomed no matter what they try. They start to feel gloomy again.

Trevor snips at Flash's feet. Flash yelps, "Ouch! Watch it with those pincers, bro!"

Trevor points a claw across the music shop floor, "Master Flash, may I suggest the stage?"

Flash looks over to a mini stage with a complete setup: guitars, drums, saxophones, bass guitars. A sign above them reads: PLEASE TRY BEFORE YOU BUY. Flash scratches his chin in thought. Then he pats Trevor's shell, "Thanks Trev!"

Trevor roars, shaking his pincer like a fist. "What is it with this shell-patting? I'm not a dog, you know!"

"Guys, come on over here to the stage." Flash runs between human legs and under a guitar stool. The other Finz follow close behind him. Trevor roars after them, shaking his pincer. All the Finz climb up onto the mini stage and are dwarfed by the size of the band instruments.

"What now, Flash mate?" asks Woody, shaking his head. "There's no way we can play these."

"Arr, Flash, look, I can't even reach the keyboard!" Sharp stands underneath the instruments on his tippy toes.

Flash smiles with confidence, "Guy's, trust me, I have a plan." Flash looks to the ceiling and punches his fist to the air. "By the

Power of Fin I command you to shrink these instruments down to size!" Flash stares at his fist then back at the instruments in shock and disappointment because nothing happens. Suddenly, a magical acid green stage-light shines over him. All the other Finz and humans in the music shop freeze.

Lord Sarrk's godly voice booms, "Flash! What is the meaning of this? You are using the Power of Fin magic in a public place?"

Flash looks to the ceiling in shame. So does Trevor. "I'm sorry, your Greatness. I just wanted to shrink these instruments down to size so we can play them. I'm using the Power of Fin magic, just like you taught me to do."

Lord Sarrk sighs. "Yes, Flash. But what about all of the humans in here? Hmm? Have you thought about that? They will all witness this strange phenomenon happen right before their very eyes. You will expose us, Flash! And what about Trevor? Did I say you could keep him as a pet? Pet monster crabs are for life you know... not just for Christmas."

Flash looks to the ceiling with a sullen face. Trevor whines with his three, sad puppy dog eyes, nodding to the ceiling. He then bares his sparkling sharp teeth, growling at Flash with an angry face.

Flash lowers his head. "Hmm, sorry, your Greatness. I didn't think of that. I just got carried away with all the excitement of having a band. We've had a bad morning so far and nothing's gone right. Can't we keep Trevor at least? Please? Just For a while longer? He's an important member of our group."

Trevor claps his pincers like castanets. "I've played with all the greats, don't you know."

Lord Sarrk ponders this notion, "Hmm, indeed. We all have our dreams of being rock stars. It seems like only the other day on planet Fin that even I was once a legend in the alien hall of rock slime fame."

"Really, your Greatness? You played?" Flash is impressed. "Wow! That must have been way cool!"

"Yes, it was, Flash, until the Alien Queen persuaded me to become a family man. Then all my rock star dreams faded away in an ocean of flat slime."

"Oh, that's a real bummer, your Greatness."

"Indeed, it was. I tell you what, I will reduce the size of these instruments for you, and I will neutralize the humans so that they do not remember seeing any of this happen when they leave, and Trevor can stay for now. We'll see if you can take care of him properly. Okay?" Trevor growls at Flash then barks like a puppy dog.

Flash's face lights up with glee. "Really? You will do that for us?"

"But of course, young Flash. I wouldn't want to stand in the way of your rock star dreams."

The lights in the music shop flicker on and off in a green smoky haze. Trevor scuttles around snapping his pincers with excitement. An acid green beam of light shoots from the ceiling, shining over the instruments. It zaps them down to size in blinding flashes. Zaaaap! Zaaap! Zaaap! Ka-POW!

The Finz jump back to life in amazement. "Wow! Flash mate, this is awesome!" cries Woody when he sits at the drums.

"Yeah Flash, you did it, man!" yells Bone, grabbing the bass.

“Come on guys, let’s jam!” Jazz and MJ stand behind the mics.

“Arr, this is truly band-tastic, Flash,” Sharp smiles, playing scales on the keyboards.

The Finz take up their instruments. Sharp on keyboards, Syke on saxophone, Woody on the drums, Bone on the bass, MJ and Jazz on backing vocals, Flash on vocals and lead guitar. Trevor the alien crab joins in on castanets. Flash stands up to the microphone and strums his guitar. All the humans in the music shop gather round the stage in sheer astonishment at the Finz’s first show.

Flash looks out at the audience, smiling broadly, “Hey everybody! We’re called the Finz, and we’re going to do a little song for you now. Remember on those days when you’re feeling down, and nothing seems to be going right? Well, you need to find something deep inside of you, that little extra strength to pick yourself back up again and carry on with your day. This extra strength is called ‘Your Inner Aussie’! So, without any further delay, here is the song, *Everybody’s got an inner Aussie bro!* Take it away guys, one, two, one, two, three, four...”

The Finz strum and drum, the saxophone blasts, and Flash bursts into the lyrics of the song:

Everybody's got an inner Aussie bro, yeah don't you know, don't yah know, everybody's got an inner Aussie bro, yeah don't you know, don't yah know. When you're feeling down and low, and there's no surf in yah flow, everybody needs an inner Aussie bro. When times are hard and you got no place to go, everybody needs an inner Aussie bro. So find your inner Aussie and pick yourself up, don't feel like you've just run right out of luck, you'll be right, keep it tight, don't go down without a fight, cause everybody's got an inner Aussie Right!..."

The crowd goes wild, cheering while the Finz continue to rock out.

Chapter Eight
Captain Rhymes

Lord Sarrk and Mode happily watch the Finz play, and hum along to the tune. They dance around the control room with contented faces. They glance at the Slurf-o-Meter, which has moved up a tiny notch.

Mode flicks some switches, turns a few dials and blasts the song from speakers outside and across the waves of planet Fin. "Let's give them a taste of this song, your Greatness. It will help build wave morale!"

"Good thinking, Mode." Lord Sarrk snaps his claws to the beat.

The alien surfers are all out in force surfing the slime on some crazy contraptions. Their gnarly faces turn slightly happier. The slime is moving ever so slightly faster now thanks to the Finz's song. The surfers of planet Fin hear the lyrics and start to hum along, too.

"Nak dak fak lak. What is an Aussie?" asks Daks.

"Flak Dak Nak. I don't know, bro. But they sure can play! Listen to that saxophone!" hums Larz.

Under the green slime waves, more underwater speakers blast the song so alien fish can hear it too. They sing along in clouds of bubbles while they swim across bright pink coral.

A fanged, alien monster rock fish with one giant cyclops eye greets a passing octopus with a transparent head. Inside the head is a smaller octopus driving the larger octopus like a space craft.

"Apparently, everyone has an inner Aussie bro," grins the monster rock fish, tapping his fins.

"Well, they are all the rage now, didn't you know?" The octopus gives a naval salute with six arms while the other two arms continue to steer.

In Trevor's house where the alien monster crab used to live, his wife is wearing a giant pink wig while knitting Trevor a crab shaped dinner suit. Even she hums along to the tune. She stares at a photo of Trevor and herself together in a loving embrace on their holidays by the beach in Mak zak dak. Trevor is holding up a bright pink drink with an umbrella in it. Trevor's wife sighs deeply, "I miss you, darling. Please come home soon..." she continues to hum the tune whilst knitting.

Back on Earth in the music shop, the Finz finish the song and get a standing ovation from the humans. The Finz take a bow and are instantly approached by a thick bearded man who smokes a pipe, wears a captain's hat, and talks like a pirate.

"Argh! That was grand! You boys and girls can sure play. You'll go a long way, argh!"

The Finz look up in surprise. Flash puts down his guitar, eyeing the stranger. "Thanks bro, but who are you?"

"Argh, Captain Rhymes is me name and signing up bands is me game. Argh."

"You sign up bands? Really? That's sick! But, do you think we're good enough?" Flash's eyes fill with hope.

"Argh, sure me does. You can sing and play, and that's why I'm signing ye up today, argh!"

The Finz look at each other in glee. "That's awesome!" They high five each other and cheer. "We did it man! Woo hoo!"

Captain Rhymes continues. “Now, if I can just get you to sign here on the dotted line, then everything will be fine...Argh...DO WE HAVE AN ACCORD?”

BUMMED NOTE
CONTRACT

The Finz's eyes pop out when they see the contract. "A million dollars?!" they shout at once.

Suddenly, acid green thunder and lightning fills the music shop. The humans and Captain Rhymes freeze. The instruments that the Finz were playing sprout back up to their normal size. Then the humans jolt back to life again, going about their day around the music shop as if nothing's happened.

"Argh, what's going on? What am I doing here?" Confused, Captain Rhymes folds the music contract away into his pocket, then puffs on his unlit pipe. He glances down at Jazz. "And who be you, me dear?"

"Captain Rhymes, you were about to sign us up to a music deal," Jazz smiles hopefully.

"I was? But I've never heard you play. So how can I say? Argh, tutti by ship-mates! Argh." Captain Rhymes walks off humming a tune.

"No, no, wait!" shouts Flash. "Captain Rhymes! Come back. Please! We..."

Suddenly there's a flicker of acid green light then Lord Sarrk's voice calls. "Flash, can you hear me? Flash? That was an incredible performance, Flashy my boy. Well done! I have neutralized the humans so they have no memory of this phenomenon ever taking place. Our secret is safe."

"No, no! Wait L'Sarrk! We were about to sign a music contract with Captain Rhymes! Please! You have to get him back we..."

"A music contract? I am afraid a neutralization of a human's memory cannot be reversed, Flash."

"But, but, no! You can't be serious? Didn't you just hear and see what Captain Rhymes said? You're supposed to be the All-Seeing Eye, right? We were about to be famous!"

"Oh? I am so sorry, Flash. I was distracted by the song, singing and dancing along and then the Alien Queen asked me to make her a cup of tea and..."

"A cupper-tea?!" Flash stares up with a disappointed face, "Mate! We were about to be rich!"

"Hey!" shouts the music shop owner, "can you guys keep it down back there? I've got customers here that can't hear themselves play badly!"

Captain Rhymes leaves the music shop, walking off down the street while humming the melody to *Everybody's Got an Inner Aussie Bro*. "Argh, now how did I gets this tune in me head? It sounds like a real winner and would make me a lot of bread! Argh." He hums, skipping his way off into the morning sun.

Chapter Nine
No More Kooks!

Back in the surf shop headquarters, the Finz admire their instruments. As an apology for losing them their million-dollar music contract, Lord Sarrk has granted them permanent band instruments, and they're just the right fit for their little finny size.

"Oh well, I guess at least we have a band now and we can practice whenever we want to." Flash admires his guitar, strumming on a string.

"Guess so," sigh Jazz and MJ.

"And it's only money, right? Mates?" Woody explains. "I mean, what's a million bucks to us? What could we do with it? Our legs are too short to drive and we don't wear any clothes."

"Yeah, yeah that's a good point, mate," nods Syke in agreement.

Without warning, a strong gale force wind blows the surf shop door open. "Take me to your surf leader," blurts a robotic voice when a strange looking creature drifts inside the surf shop and the door slams behind it.

"What the...?" The Finz stare at the giant bright purple barnacle that hovers off the ground with a cyclops eye. Tentacles drift off the back of its head like dreadlocks. It moves as if it's still underwater.

"Take me to your surf leader," repeats the barnacle in a robotic voice.

"Surf what, mate?" asks Flash, doing a double-take.

"Take me to your surf leader. I am wanting to surf."

Syke drops his shades, revealing the tops of his bright green eyes. "Whoa bro, that's a barney looking kook man!"

"What is the meaning of kook?" asks the barnacle floating further into the room. His giant eye revolves around the surf shop, eyeing up all the boards. "My name is Salzac."

"A kook is a human that thinks he can surf, mate," explains Woody. But he can't, and you got no arms."

"You mean these?" Salzac sprouts giant purple hands then arms from out of his shell. He grabs one of the Finz's surfboards. "I'm no kook. I can out-surf you any time! Now, take me to your surf leader."

"Whoo, that's freaky, man," whispers Bone. "Dude's got magic hands."

"Okay, okay so you think you can surf. So what? And we don't have a surf leader, bro," shrugs Flash. "No one's in charge. We just surf whenever we want too."

"No leader?" Salzac asks in surprise. "Who is keeping order in the waves?"

"This freaky alien dude's got a good point," Sharp admits with admiration. "We need a wave referee with those hairy headed kooks dropping in. Arrr."

Salzac nods in agreement. "We have this problem on our planet. If you drop in on another surfer you get vaporised."

CLOSED
LET'S GO SURFING

"Hmm, sounds good." Flash rubs his chin, remembering the last kook that ruined his wave. He imagines the kook being zapped from the ocean.

Suddenly, the shop door bursts open. "Hey, Shane mate, surf's up!" shouts Shane's mate Wayne from outside.

Shane, the surf shop owner, grabs his board and runs out the shop after posting a note on the door saying he'll be back in two hours.

"Did you hear that, man?" grins Bone. "The waves are back!"

"Arrrr!" Let's hit the green room guys, come on!" Sharp races outside.

"Akaw!" Jazz punches her fist.

"Surf's up, Charlie!" shouts MJ. "Let's go!"

The Finz snatch their boards and run out the door. Flash looks at the floating barnacle. "Hey guys wait! What about this floating alien dude?"

"They said surf's up, let's move!" Salzac's eye widens and he pulls a laser gun from his shell. "And the name is Salzac, but you can call me Sal."

Flash's eyes widen with concern, "No, wait bro! What are you doing? Put that thing away. You can't just go around lasering humans that can't surf on Bondi." Flash thinks again, "No you can't! But...er, um... maybe...No! Just no!"

Salzac reluctantly hides the laser gun back in his shell. "Okay, but please can I surf with you? I have not surfed since beaming to your planet and I'm getting rather clucky."

Flash sighs, "Okay, okay, but no laser guns, Sal!"

"Agreed," Salzac promises.

At Bondi beach, the afternoon sun shines brightly while fun waves roll in. The Finz are all surfing, but the crowds are also building. Someone drops in on Syke and he yells, "Hey, hey stop!"

"Sorry," calls a human voice.

"Sorry? You were looking right at me, you hairy headed kook!"

"Man, it's so busy out here," complains Bone paddling over to Syke.

"Arrr, it's not surf-chi-tastic guys. It's crowd-nastic!" Sharp pouts.

"Look out!" Jazz yells when a kook cuts her off. "That's the second time!"

"Sorry, man," shouts another human.

Flash paddles over to them with Sal beside him. A large shark fin follows then circles around them all. "Guys, this is ridiculous. There are just too many humans out here. What are we going to do?"

"Maybe I can help," suggests Salzac in his robot voice, pulling out the laser gun again.

"Whoa, dude. That's a bit aggro." Syke raises his eyebrows with concern.

The shark fin swims over to Salzac. Then Mr. Chompy Chomps pops his head out of the water growling at him like a guard dog.

"Bro!" snaps Flash at Salzac, "what did I tell you back in the surf shop? We can't just go around smoking kooks!" The others think about it for a second as the waves fall silent. "No! We can't! Can we?" Flash hears another clash of boards.

Mr. Chompy Chomps whines then ducks back under and continues to circle the Finz.

"I have an idea," Salzac raises his eyebrow and cocks his laser.

The Finz gulp. "I can adjust the settings on this to only stun and zap. Not vaporise."

"Stun and zap?" they all shriek at once.

"Yes. If I turn this dial here it will only stun then zap the kooks back to the last thing they were doing before they went for a surf."

Flash rubs his chin, thinking about it. "And none of the kooks will be harmed?"

"Nope," Salzac's one eye drifts to the left, "at least I don't think so."

"You don't think?!" MJ holds her hands up.

"STOP!" They all hear a human shout, "Get off my wave!"

"Okay," they all nod, "let's do it!"

Salzac's eye turns cunning, then he sprouts arms and paddles onto a wave. A human surfer drops in on him. He draws his laser and fires, "*Hasta la vista*, baby!" Zap! Zap! Zap! Ka-POW! The surfer jolts, disappearing in an acid green puff of smoke!

"Oops!" Flash looks to the others. "That doesn't sound good, bros. And he's talking like Arnold Schwarzenegger too."

"Argh!" The dripping wet surfer zaps back in front of his computer. His surfboard slams on his desk. He shrieks in confusion, "What the...?"

Salzac continues to zap more human surfers that drop in on the Finz's waves. "I'll be back." Zap! Ka-POW! "Bite me. You're toast. You've just been erased, kook." He blows into his laser then holsters it back in his shell.

Another human surfer finds himself back in bed soaking wet and cuddling up to his board sucking his thumb.

Salzac paddles over to the Finz with a happy face. All the kooks have gone.

"Wow, man!" exclaims Bone. "We've got Bondi nearly all to ourselves!"

"Amped!" shouts Jazz, catching a wave and riding it all the way to the end.

"Stoked!" cries MJ doing the same. "This is epic!"

"Radical, Sal! But mate," Flash wonders, "how do you know about Arnold Schwarzenegger?"

"Since our planets became connected we have been downloading all of your earth movies. I am a big fan of Arnie. *Hasta la vista*, baby!" Salzac pulls his laser gun, swivelling it in his hands and does Arnie impressions.

The Finz all crack up, laughing, "*Hasta la vista*, kooks!"

Mr. Chompy Chomps breaches, happily gnashing his gleaming teeth. Suddenly, dark clouds roll in and flicker in pulses of light. Then a green cone hones in on Salzac and pulls him up out of the ocean into a vortex. He swirls around and around up into the clouds.

"I'll be back," he calls down to the Finz while they all look up and wave goodbye. He vanishes in a zap of light.

Then Lord Sarrk's voice booms, "Flash! What is the meaning of this? The ocean is for everyone to use! It's not just for you and your finny friends!"

Flash looks up to dark clouds and blushes, "I'm sorry, your Greatness. We just got carried away. It was Sal's idea. He led us on, but we didn't mean it."

"Salzac will be punished for his actions, young finny boy, and you and your friends must promise to never to do this again. Do you understand? Because of your negative actions the Slurf-o-Meter has dropped, wasting all of our hard work. If there's any more of this behaviour, you shall be banished to planet Fin forever."

Flash gulps. "We promise, your Greatness."

"Very well, then." Lord Sarrk's voice fades away. The clouds clear and the afternoon sun shines its warm rays.

"Well, me old mates, Sal's been erased." Flash paddles after a wave. "We better be more careful next time, or we're all be banished to some distant planet with slimy waves and no tacos."

The Finz nod in agreement that Bondi is for everyone to enjoy.

"Rad Power!" Shouts Flash, riding off into the sun. Mr. Chompy Chomps races after him.

FIN

BUT, TO BE CONTINUED...

I hope you enjoyed this first book in the series of the Bondi Finz, as there are lots more to come. If you did enjoy the show, please leave a review on Amazon or the eBook platform from where you downloaded the book. It means a lot and really helps me as an emerging author.

Thank you,

Simon.

Also, please check out my author central page on Amazon, where you'll find all my other books and author updates: https://amzn.to/2GxhQpC.

THE BONDI FINZ™

More Bondi Finz adventures

Planet Fin's gnarly, alien inhabitants love nothing more than to surf the waves of their oceans. But they did not take care of their environment and the surf turned into a green slimy gunk called slurf. Yuk! They develop a bio beam to rejuvenate the slurf, but the laser misfires. The beam ricochets around the galaxies before zapping Earth through a surf shop window in Bondi, Sydney, Australia, where a row of surfboard fins are displayed. ZAP! KAPOW! The Finz burst to life! Seven knee-high, radical characters begin an epic adventure on a quest for the holy grail of surf.

Will the Finz find out why they were created? Will they help the alien leader to save Planet Fin's surf? Read on, groms! And big groms at heart too!

Book Two: Shark Frog

Have you had your head polished lately? Have you ever been to a surf tailor? With their fins freshly polished and fitted out with new, extravagant rides, the Bondi Finz sure have. They're back again with more surf-mayhem adventures.

Flash finds himself sucked through alien portholes while Mr. Chompy Chomps gets the shock of his shark life. And Bondi's dogs receive an unexpected aggro barney makeover!

A new king is in town and Bondi is about to be attacked by something gnarly, bro! Lord Sarrk and Mode desperately try to stop the invasion.

Will love and a crab-shaped dinner suit save the day!?

Book Three: FreeRacer

Can you say that you love and respect kooks? The Finz might have to. Plastics in the ocean are definitely slowing down the motion! The Finz must find a way to clean the sea and beach and make it plastic-FREE! But this will only happen if Lord Sarrk and Mode can destroy Trevor's gnarly virus and restore Zoid powers in time.

Flash finds himself in a sticky wax dilemma – he needs a FreeForma surf skate bike and makes a surfboard deal with Syke that he cannot keep.

Meanwhile, the race is on. But this is no ordinary competition. Flash and Syke battle it out with the hairy headed humans on the FreeRacer track. Sliding, wave-riding, and freestyling. Who will win? I don't know. Read on to enjoy the show!

Book Four: Surf Subs

Do you speak Dolphinian, bro? More amped Finz antics return where surf subs are go, go, go when the baby Finz spring into action! Bubble wobble on the baby double! Maaaaate!

And just like Jurassic Park, nature finds a way. Eggs have been laid. But by whom? And Flash thinks Eco shark nets are a Rad Power must.

Bone gets a new, one-eyed tooth-crunching buddy while it's shipmates, me hearties! Captain Rhymes sails all the way to Bali... but on a longboard. What!?

Meanwhile, something extraterrestrial has hijacked Flash's surf school and it's definitely NOT shaka, bro! What will happen? I don't know! Read all about it if you want to see the epic conclusion!

Please surf over to my website www.sjhouse.com.au and sign up to my mailing list, where you'll be notified when more Bondi Finz adventures are out and much, much more. I promise, you will not be spammed!

All my best

Simon.

S J House
AUTHOR BIOGRAPHY

Simon was born in London. Despite being dyslexic, he has always been highly creative with a strong and vivid imagination. With a background in never-before-seen product design (including his FreeForma surf skate bike invention), Simon lives in Sydney, Australia, where his passions are surfing and writing. Indeed, his first series, *Andee The Aquanaut*, developed from a character he created while in the water! The series won an independent author award.

Simon constantly seeks new and creative forms of expression. He loves to write at a fast pace with never a dull moment and has discovered that writing for kids gives him the thrill he seeks.

With his enthusiasm for make believe, and creating new ideas for characters and superheroes, he feels *the sky's the limit*;

there's so much one can tune into. This excitement motivates him to create inspiring works that are original and innovative, sparking the reader's imagination, taking them on journeys into amazing worlds.

Simon's second series, titled *Menosaurus*, has the same amount of action, an equally adventurous hero, and shocking villains, this series takes place both on Earth and in the depths of space. A race of super-intelligent dinosaur humanoids plot to reclaim Earth, which they believe to be rightfully theirs. The incredible illustrations are created by renowned, award-winning illustrator, Zoran Zlaticanin.

Most recently, Simon has completed *Grey Squirrels London*, a humorous and fast-paced animal adventure for junior readers. Following the hair-raising and hysterical adventures of six squirrels, on a quest across London, England, this novel encourages readers to consider the oneness of all living beings.

Simon supports various conservation orgs that are marine and rhino-related, through the sales of his books. With Simon, it seems that anything that's *way out there* is actually deep within.

For more info, interviews, and reviews, check out the web address below.

www.sjhouse.com.au